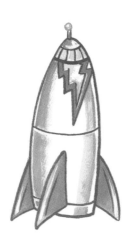

**Give your child a head start with
PICTURE READERS**

Dear Parent,

Now children as young as preschool age can have the fun and satisfaction of reading a book all on their own.

In every Picture Reader, there are simple words, rebus pictures, and 24 flash cards to cut out and keep. (There is a flash card for every rebus picture plus extra cards for reading practice.) After children listen to each story a couple of times, they will be ready to try it all by themselves.

Collect all the titles in our Picture Reader series. Once children have mastered these books, they can move on to Levels 1, 2, and 3 in our All Aboard Reading series.

ISBN 0-448-41566-6      D E F G H I J

A PICTURE READER

**By Roberta Edwards**
**Illustrated by Nate Evans**

Grosset & Dunlap • New York

Hi! I live way out

in space.

I can see the

and the

far, far away.

I get out of .

I put on my

and my .

Now I can go

and play.

I go to the

next door.

My  comes too.

I play with my friend.

My  plays

with his .

We all have fun.

We ride

our jet .

ZOOM!

Off we go.

We stop

at the park.

We go on the

and the .

I look at my .

Oh! It is late.

I must go back

to my .

Mom, Dad,

and the

are getting into

our .

I am just in time.

We are going

to get .

The  goes by

lots of

and .

Then we stop.

We all have .

I have extra

and

on my .

Later we fly home.

I am sleepy.

I get in  .

I read a  —

a scary  .

It is about kids on 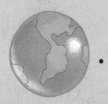 .

But I know

it is just a story.

After all, there

are no kids on  .

| earth | sun |
|-------|-----|
| shirt | bed |
| house | pants |

| bike | dog |
|------|-----|
| slide | swings |
| baby | watch |

| pizza | rocket |
| --- | --- |
| stars | moon |
| cheese | mushrooms |

| tree | book |
|------|------|
| ball | pig |
| seesaw | cat |